Welcome to ALADDIN QUIX!

If you are looking for fast, fun-to-read stories with colorful characters, lots of kid-friendly humor, easy-to-follow action, entertaining story lines, and lively illustrations, then **ALADDIN QUIX** is for you!

But wait, there's more!

If you're also looking for stories with tables of contents; word lists; about-the-book questions; 64, 80, or 96 pages; short chapters; short paragraphs; and large fonts, then **ALADDIN QUIX** is *definitely* for you!

ALADDIN QUIX: The next step between ready to reads and longer, more challenging chapter books, for readers five to eight years old.

Read more ALADDIN QUIX books!

By Stephanie Calmenson

Our Principal Is a Frog!
Our Principal Is a Wolf!
Our Principal's in His Underwear!
Our Principal Breaks a Spell!
Our Principal's Wacky Wishes!
Our Principal Is a Spider!
Our Principal Is a Scaredy-Cat!
Our Principal Is a Noodlehead!

The Adventures of Allie and Amy
By Stephanie Calmenson and Joanna Cole

Book 1: *The Best Friend Plan*
Book 2: *Rockin' Rockets*
Book 3: *Stars of the Show*
Book 4: *Costume Parade*

ADDY McBEAN #2

Time Out!

BY
Margery Cuyler

ILLUSTRATED BY
Stacy Curtis

ALADDIN QUIX

New York   Amsterdam/Antwerp   London   Toronto   Sydney   New Delhi

To Jan, who gets everywhere ten minutes ahead of time
—M. C.

For Maddy, Olivia, and Nora
—S. C.

This book is a work of fiction. Any references to historical events, real people, or real places are used fictitiously. Other names, characters, places, and events are products of the author's imagination, and any resemblance to actual events or places or persons, living or dead, is entirely coincidental.

ALADDIN QUIX
Simon & Schuster Children's Publishing Division
1230 Avenue of the Americas, New York, New York 10020
First Aladdin QUIX hardcover edition January 2025
Text copyright © 2025 by Margery Cuyler
Illustrations copyright © 2025 by Stacy Curtis
Also available in an Aladdin QUIX paperback edition.
All rights reserved, including the right of reproduction in whole or in part in any form.
ALADDIN and the related marks and colophon are trademarks of Simon & Schuster, LLC.
For information about special discounts for bulk purchases, please contact Simon & Schuster Special Sales at 1-866-506-1949 or business@simonandschuster.com.
The Simon & Schuster Speakers Bureau can bring authors to your live event.
For more information or to book an event contact the Simon & Schuster Speakers Bureau at 1-866-248-3049 or visit our website at www.simonspeakers.com.
Designed by Laura Lyn DiSiena
The illustrations for this book were rendered digitally.
The text of this book was set in Archer Medium.
Manufactured in the United States of America 1224 LAK
2 4 6 8 10 9 7 5 3 1
Library of Congress Cataloging-in-Publication Data
Names: Cuyler, Margery, author. | Curtis, Stacy, illustrator. Title: Time out! / by Margery Cuyler ; illustrated by Stacy Curtis. Description: First Aladdin hardcover/paperback edition 2025. | New York : Aladdin, 2025. | Series: Addy McBean ; 2 | Audience: Ages 5 to 8 | Summary: Second-grader Addy McBean loves numbers, but lately she has started loving learning about clocks, watches, and anything that tells time. Identifiers: LCCN 2024033499 (print) | LCCN 2024033500 (ebook) | ISBN 9781534489592 (paperback) | ISBN 9781534489608 (hardcover) | ISBN 9781534489615 (ebook) Subjects: CYAC: Time—Fiction. | Mathematics—Fiction. Classification: LCC PZ7.C997 Ti 2025 (print) | LCC PZ7.C997 (ebook) | DDC Fic]—dc23
LC record available at https://lccn.loc.gov/2024033499
LC ebook record available at https://lccn.loc.gov/2024033500

Cast of Characters

Addy McBean: Second grader at PS 8 who loves numbers

Mom: Addy's mother; librarian at South Summit Public Library

Minus: Addy's dog

Willard Gluck: Addy's classmate

Mr. Vertex: Addy's teacher at PS 8

Star Atlas: Addy's best friend

Maya: Addy's classmate

Jamie: Addy's classmate

Ms. Atlas: Star's mother; works at PS 8

Mr. Rogers: Gym teacher at PS 8

Dad: Addy's dad; coding genius who lives in San Francisco

Leo: Addy's classmate

Akim: Addy's classmate

Ms. Tempo: Music teacher at PS 8

Latoya: Addy's classmate

Collin: Addy's classmate

Mr. Gluck: Willard's father

Mita: Addy's classmate

Maria: Addy's classmate

Linda: Addy's classmate

Carlos: Addy's classmate

Ms. Artuso: Jamie's mother

Luna Bright: Famous pop singer

Ms. Ralston: Principal at PS 8

Contents

Chapter 1: Sequined Boots   1
Chapter 2: A New Clue   14
Chapter 3: Addy's Brainstorm   25
Chapter 4: News Spreads   33
Chapter 5: Alarming Alarms   40
Chapter 6: Field Trip   46
Chapter 7: The Nick of Time   55
Chapter 8: Time's Up!   66
Word List   79
Questions   82

1

Sequined Boots

Addy McBean lives with **Mom** and their poodle, **Minus**, at 100 Division Drive, South Summit, New Jersey. Addy is wild about numbers.

When she's not counting stuff,

she's doing addition and subtraction in her head.

She likes to skip count by tens to one thousand. The other second graders can't do this yet, except for **Willard Gluck**. He's a math whiz too. They have fun skip counting together.

Addy is in **Mr. Vertex**'s class at PS 8. Math is the first class of the day. It's Mr. Vertex's favorite subject. He wears ties with numbers on them and shoes with math objects.

On Monday morning Mr. Vertex greets Addy and her best friend, **Star Atlas**, with a riddle.

"What works every day, every hour, every minute, and every second?"

Addy usually comes up with an answer, but today she's **stumped**.

"I don't know," she says.

Star doesn't either, so Mr. Vertex exclaims, "**A clock!** In math today we'll begin a new unit on how to tell time."

Addy already knows how, since she has a smart watch and can read the time on the front. Her dad gave it to her when he moved to San Francisco after her parents got divorced. When Addy's not in school, she and her dad text back and forth all the time.

After the Pledge of Allegiance, Mr. Vertex makes the V sign for everyone to be quiet. Then he holds up a clock that shows the time on a **rectangular** screen.

"I bet this clock looks familiar," he says. "Does anyone know what kind of clock it is?"

Willard raises his hand. "A **digital clock**, and the time reads eight thirty-seven." *Of course Willard knows the answer. His mom and dad are astrophysicists. They've taught him lots about numbers and outer space,* thinks Addy.

Mr. Vertex explains that the

number before the **colon** marks the hour. The numbers after the colon mark the minutes. Addy yawns. She and some of the other kids already know this. Next their teacher points to the round clock on the wall.

"What kind of clock is that?"

Maya raises her hand. "A full-moon clock," she says.

"Good guess," says Mr. Vertex, "since it's round like a full moon. But it's called an **analog clock**." He explains that analog clocks have round faces and three hands that

travel in the same direction. The numbers on the clock's face stand for hours. The little lines between the numbers stand for minutes. The small hand points to the number that tells what hour it is. The big hand tells the number of minutes that have passed in the hour.

"What does the skinny hand do?" asks **Jamie**.

"It tells how many seconds have gone by," explains Mr. Vertex. He continues, "It's important to learn how to tell time. It will help you stay organized. I'll give out math sheets for your homework. They include exercises to help you learn to read a clock. We'll play some time games in class, too."

A few students roll their eyes at the thought of so much homework.

Even though Addy knows what time it is on her smart watch, she realizes there's a lot more to discover. *The more I learn, the more organized I'll be. I like to know when things happen and how long things take.*

After the last bell, Addy and Star go to meet Star's mom. **Ms. Atlas** works in the main office and drives the two girls to and from school every day.

As Addy and Star follow Ms. Atlas through the parking lot, they pass Mr. Vertex's little blue car.

Something sparkly catches Addy's eye. She looks into a front window. A pair of **sequined** boots is lying on the passenger seat. *What is Mr. Vertex doing with those?* she wonders.

"Star, come quick," she yells.

"Wow," says Star, looking into the car. "Those boots are beautiful."

"I wonder who they belong to," Addy muses. "Maybe to a friend or another teacher. Or maybe"—she pauses—"Mr. Vertex has a girlfriend!"

"That would be cool," says Star.

Addy's silent for a moment, then says, "The other day I heard him mention a reception to **Mr. Rogers**, the gym teacher. What if he was talking about a wedding reception? **Countabunga!** I wonder if he's getting married!"

"Countabunga" is Addy's favorite expression.

"I'm not so sure," says Star. "The boots could be a present for someone. What if we ask him?"

"No," says Addy. "He might get

mad if he thinks we've been snooping. But if he *is* getting married, I hope he'll invite our class to the wedding."

Addy's eyes sparkle.

2

A New Clue

When Addy gets home, she walks Minus and then texts her dad.

Addy to **Dad**:

Mr. Vertex is teaching us how to tell time.

Right now my watch says it's 4:05.

What time is it in San Francisco?

Dad to Addy:

It's 1:05. Three hours behind your time, as always.

That's because I'm in a different time zone.

Addy to Dad:

I find time zones confusing.

Dad to Addy:

It's hard to explain them in a text.

You can look them up on the computer.

Addy to Dad:

Or I can just ask my friend Willard. He knows everything.

Guess what? Mr. Vertex might be getting married.

Stay tuned for more info.

Dad to Addy:

Keep me posted.

Addy sends Dad a photo of Minus and puts her phone away.

In twenty-five minutes, it will be yoga time with Mom. Every afternoon Addy and Mom practice their poses while watching a yoga video.

As Addy waits for her mother to come downstairs, she grabs a piece of paper and a marker. She sits at the kitchen counter and writes down a **schedule** of her day.

When Addy finishes her list, she tapes it to the fridge door.

At 4:25, Mom comes into the kitchen wearing a T-shirt with a **lotus** flower on it.

She stops and stares at Addy's schedule.

"My goodness, Addy! That's quite a list," she says.

"We're learning how to tell time in school, so I'm practicing."

"Let's count how many seconds we breathe in and out as we do our poses," says Mom. "I'll also get you some books about telling time."

Addy's mom is a librarian at the South Summit Public Library. She brings home lots of different books for Addy to read.

< >

The next day Mr. Vertex shares a number of time facts.

He also asks Willard to sit on a chair in front of the class.

"I want you to pretend you're asleep," he says. "When it's time for you to wake up, I'll clap. Then your classmates will look at the analog wall clock and tell me what time you woke up."

Willard starts to snore and then **mutters** nonsense, as if he's having

a dream. When Mr. Vertex claps, everyone glances at the clock.

"Eight ten," yells **Leo**.

"Nine ten," cries Maya.

"Eight twelve and five seconds," shouts Willard, which of course is the right answer.

By the end of the next week, the students can tell time on both analog and digital clocks. They've also learned how to set alarms. Addy has been so busy studying time, she almost forgot about her teacher and his *maybe* getting-married plans.

When it's time for science, Mr. Vertex writes the three Rs, "Reduce, Reuse, Recyle" on the board attached to the wall. Then he asks Addy and **Akim** to move the class's recycling container to below the three Rs. Addy notices a note taped to the bookshelf above Mr. Vertex's desk. It says CATERING with a bunch of phone numbers scrawled beneath it.

Countabunga! Another clue! Mr. Vertex is checking out the food for the reception. That means he MUST be getting married!

When school's over, Addy tells Star about the note.

"That doesn't really prove anything," says Star. "Mr. Vertex could be planning a birthday party or something."

"I guess you might be right," says Addy. "But let's keep watching for more clues."

3

Addy's Brainstorm

Twice a month, on Thursdays, Mr. Vertex's second-grade class has music in place of library time.

Addy looks forward to this class because she likes counting the beats to the songs.

As the students file into the music room, their teacher, **Ms. Tempo**, greets them with a smile. She has on black leggings covered with musical notes and is wearing purple suede boots. A sparkly barrette is clipped into her bouncy red hair.

Once everyone has sat cross-legged on the rug, Ms. Tempo puts her hands on her head to get the class's attention. "I have something unusual to share with you today," she says. "Mr. Vertex and I have worked together on a song about numbers. He wrote the words, and I wrote the music." She waves some papers in the air. "I'll pass out the **lyrics**. Mr. Vertex wrote them for a special occasion."

A special occasion! Could it be the occasion I'm hoping for? Addy wonders, as she starts reading the words.

From zero to infinity,

Numbers are a symphony.

Tell the time on different clocks,

Count your markers, count your socks.
Count the hours in a day,
Count the minutes as you play.
From zero to infinity,
Numbers are a symphony.

Ms. Tempo presses her purple suede boots to the piano pedals and sings the song all the way through.

BRAIN FLASH! BRAIN FLASH! BRAIN FLASH!

What if Ms. Tempo is Mr. V's girlfriend? She wears a barrette that matches the sequined boots. She and

Mr. Vertex worked together on the song, thinks Addy. *They both wear fun clothes, and they're both teachers. They're a perfect match.*

Addy can't wait to talk to Star. As they walk to the swings during

afternoon recess, she shares her brainstorm with her BFF.

"I guess Ms. Tempo *could* be Mr. Vertex's girlfriend," admits Star. "But we still don't know for sure. Maybe other kids in our class know something we don't. I'll ask **Latoya** if she's heard anything. And my mom, too."

"I'll ask Willard," says Addy.

< >

At 8:09 a.m. the following morning, Mr. Vertex has a new riddle for the two friends.

"Can you make ten plus four equal two?"

Addy thinks for a minute, then answers, "Ten o'clock plus four hours equals two o'clock."

"Excellent!" exclaims Mr. Vertex.

"We really like your numbers song," says Star.

Mr. Vertex blushes. Addy thinks that must mean something. "I had fun writing it, and Ms. Tempo did a fantastic job with the music."

At the end of the school day,

Mr. Vertex tells the class, "Next Wednesday we are going on a field trip. We'll walk along Main Street to hunt for clocks. We'll also do some fun math along the way."

Mr. V continues, "We'll end our trip at Marvel Park, where **Collin**'s mom will meet us with pizzas. And . . . I have a surprise that I'll share with you that day."

Addy's heart leaps into her throat. Finally he will tell us his BIG NEWS. Addy looks over at Star and mouths, *It's time!* and gives her a thumbs-up.

4

News Spreads

On Saturday at 1:49 p.m., Willard calls Addy and invites her over to play chess. Chess is Addy's favorite game. Sometimes she even beats Willard. She hops onto her bike and rides to his condo five streets away. She arrives by 2:04 p.m.

As they set up the chessboard in Willard's kitchen, **Mr. Gluck** pours them each a mug of hot chocolate and sets out four star-shaped cookies. Then he disappears to do **research** on asteroids.

After Addy moves her **pawn**, she asks, "Have you heard anything

about Mr. V getting married?"

"Huh?" says Willard. "What makes you think that?"

Addy explains what she and Star have pieced together.

"I get why Ms. Tempo would like his flashy ties and cool shoes," says Willard. "But I haven't heard anything about a wedding." He moves his knight. "Checkmate," he exclaims, ending the game and any more questions from Addy.

The minute Addy gets home, she calls Star and reports that Willard hasn't heard any rumors.

Star says, "My mom thinks we shouldn't jump to conclusions about Mr. Vertex's personal life." Star adds that Latoya also has heard nothing.

"That's too bad," exclaims Addy. "A wedding would be awesome."

"I guess that's the end of it," remarks Star.

But it turns out, that isn't quite the end of it. After talking to Star, Latoya called Maya, who called **Mita**, who called **Maria**, and the news spread like spilled juice.

< >

At recess on Monday, Maya says, "Last week, when I was waiting to be picked up in the front office, guess what happened? A big bunch of balloons was delivered to Mr. Vertex."

Another clue! thinks Addy.

"When do you suppose the wedding will take place?" asks **Linda**.

"Where will they go on their honeymoon?" wonders Jamie.

"They should spend it at Cinco Ranch in Texas," says **Carlos**.

"I bet Ms. Tempo's wedding dress will have musical notes on it!" exclaims Mita.

Addy's heart feels jumpy. *What have Star and I started? People's imaginations are going wild. I HOPE, HOPE, HOPE that Mr. Vertex's surprise on field trip day will be an announcement about getting married. Otherwise, if it's not true and he hears the rumor, he might get mad. If only things could be as predictable as telling time.*

5

Alarming Alarms

On the night before the field trip, Addy runs around the house collecting clocks. She carries two analog and three digital clocks to her bedroom and lays them on her desk. She plugs in the digital clocks and checks the batteries on the analog ones. Then she sets all the alarms for 6:00 a.m. the next morning. Getting up forty-five minutes earlier than usual will give her plenty of time to prepare for the day.

At 6:00 a.m. all the alarms go off at once.

The wake-up song on Addy's bedside clock, "One, Two, Three! I'm Awake!" also starts playing.

Mom rushes into the room in her pj's, covering her ears with her hands.

"What's going on?" she cries. She snatches one of the analog clocks and switches off the sound. Addy scrambles out of bed and stops the other alarms.

"What were you thinking?" asks Mom.

"I didn't want to oversleep. I'm getting up extra early to prepare and organize for the field trip." *And for more than just the field trip,* Addy thinks.

"Too much, too noisy, too loud!" yells Mom.

Addy runs over to her mom and gives her a hug. "I'm sorry," she says. "I didn't think the alarms would sound so horrible."

Mom hugs her back. "All right. Just please promise me one thing. Don't ever do that again!"

After Mom leaves the room, Addy runs down to the kitchen. She stuffs her backpack with crackers, pretzels, and health bars. She adds a few Band-Aids in case she gets a blister. She throws in an umbrella as well, if it rains. She rushes back upstairs, brushes her teeth, and puts on her favorite hoody, with the number one hundred on it. She glances at her clock. It's 6:40 a.m., twenty-eight minutes until breakfast. She decides to text Dad, even though it's 3:40 a.m. in San Francisco.

Addy to Dad:

Today Mr. V is taking us on a field trip.

We'll walk into town, look for clocks, and do some fun math.

Mr. Vertex told us he has a surprise to share. Maybe he'll tell us his BIG NEWS about getting married.

Time to go—lol!

Addy takes a picture of the clocks on her desk and sends it to Dad.

6

Field Trip

When Addy gets to school, she and Star are happy and relieved to find out they get to be

field trip partners. The class follows Mr. Vertex to the flagpole in front of the school, where **Ms. Artuso**, Jamie's mother, joins them as the parent helper.

Mr. Vertex announces, "You know the rules: Stay with your partner. Don't leave the line. No pushing. No running. Now, how many minutes do you think it will take for us to walk to town?" he asks.

Willard, who has Linda as his partner,

answers, "Twelve point five minutes, thirty-nine point four seconds."

Mr. Vertex laughs and says, "That's very **precise**, Willard. Let's just round it off to twelve minutes, and you can keep track."

Twelves minutes later, with Willard smiling broadly, the group stops at the Smart Fitness Studio.

The sign on the door reads:

Monday–Friday 6:00 a.m.–11:00 p.m.

Saturday 8:00 a.m.–6:00 p.m.

Sunday 12:00 p.m.–6:00 p.m.

Mr. Vertex asks, "How many hours

is the studio open on Sundays?"

Latoya calls out, **"Six."**

"Correct," says Mr. Vertex. "How many minutes are in an hour?"

"Sixty," says Collin.

"How many minutes are in six hours?"

Addy does the math in her head. *Sixty plus sixty plus sixty plus sixty plus sixty plus sixty.*

"Three hundred and sixty," she cries. She can't believe she beat Willard to the answer.

As they continue their walk,

Mr. Vertex explains that children their age take roughly one hundred and ten steps in a minute. The students start counting their steps and estimate how many minutes it takes to reach each stop. Finally they pause by the historic clock in front of Connie's Cupcakes. Its round face sits on top of a tall, old-fashioned pole stuck into the sidewalk. It's surrounded by a fence that's covered with posters and ads.

Mr. Vertex explains, "This clock

was made in 1897. It's called a street clock. A lot of old towns have historic clocks on their main streets."

Star and Addy are standing near the fence that surrounds the clock's pole. Suddenly Star jabs Addy in the ribs. "Look!" She points to a poster that shows a young woman in sequined boots. She has on a sequined jacket and is singing into a microphone. The poster says:

LUNA BRIGHT IN CONCERT

SUNDAY, DEC. 2

1:30–4:30 P.M.

STARLIGHT BALLROOM

10 JEFFERSON AVE.

SOUTH SUMMIT, NJ

"Those boots are just like the ones in Mr. Vertex's car. Wait a minute! It's not Ms. Tempo he's engaged to. It must be the pop star he's engaged to. **And there's the proof!**" exclaims Addy.

Just then Mr. Vertex gestures for the class to gather around him. "It's time to share my surprise," he says, a big grin on his face.

The second graders hold their breaths. Addy and Star lean forward. *Is this it? Is he going to tell us about the wedding?*

"I've ordered two dozen cupcakes for our picnic. Some are chocolate, others are vanilla, a few are gluten-free, and all have frosting with different times written on top," he says before entering the store.

Addy loves cupcakes, but Mr. Vertex's surprise isn't what she expected or wanted to hear.

"I can't stand the suspense any

longer," she tells Star. "We *HAVE* to learn if all the clues add up. Let's ask Mr. Vertex at the picnic if he's getting married."

"Are you sure?" says Star in a trembly voice. "This whole thing is making me nervous. Really nervous. My mom warned me that we shouldn't jump to conclusions."

"Even so, it's time to learn the truth!" declares Addy.

7
The Nick of Time

When they get to Marvel Park, Collin's mom is already there with four boxes of pizzas. She has set three tables with orange tablecloths, paper plates, and juice boxes.

As everyone gobbles down their

pizza, Mr. Vertex challenges his students with another math problem.

"The dogs at a dog show perform every four hours. Their first show ended at noon. What times are their next two shows?"

"Four o'clock and eight o'clock?" says Akim.

"A.m. or p.m.?" asks Mr. Vertex.

Akim is quiet for a moment. Then he says, "I think p.m., because noon is in the middle of the day."

"Good job!" says Mr. Vertex.

After lunch their teacher announces

that the students can play until 1:45 p.m., when it will be time to walk back to school. The second graders spread out and climb on the jungle gym, the seesaws, and the swings. Collin and Carlos throw a Frisbee back and forth. Akim settles beneath a tree and reads a book. Mr. Vertex and the parents sit at a picnic table and chat as they watch the students play.

Addy grips Star's arm. "Now we should ask him. Let's go." Addy's heart skips beats as the two girls approach their teacher.

"Star and I need to speak to you alone," says Addy.

"Sure," answers Mr. Vertex. "Let's sit on the bench near the sandbox."

Once they're settled, Addy takes a deep breath. *Here goes.* She takes a second deep breath, then blurts out, "Are you getting married?"

Mr. Vertex looks **startled**. His eyebrows rise to the middle of his forehead. For a moment he doesn't say anything. Then with a frown he asks, "Whatever gave you that idea? The answer is no."

Addy and Star interrupt each other as they sum up all the clues. They end by mentioning the poster with **Luna Bright** in the sequined boots.

"Our class thinks you're getting married," says Star.

"It's kind of our fault, right, Addy?"

Addy's cheeks start to turn red. Then she clears her throat, hoping her voice still works even if her face is on fire. "I'm sorry."

"Me too," whispers Star.

"We really misread the clues," says Addy. "And I guess it's none of our business whether you're getting married... or not."

"You guess right," says Mr. Vertex. His eyebrows drop back into their usual position. "Still," he continues, "you did the right thing by coming and talking to me. I know you didn't mean any harm. But it's important to find out the facts, so rumors don't start and spread. I'll put a stop to this rumor right now!"

He stands up and blows his whistle, **beckoning** the students to come over. After he makes the V sign and has everyone's attention, he begins, "I understand there's a rumor going around that I'm getting married."

The students start whispering.

"Well, it's not true," he continues. "Sometimes rumors get started because people overhear or even make up things without checking the facts. Then one thing leads to another, and false news spreads." He clears his throat and goes on to explain, "The balloons I received were congratulations for an article I wrote about making math fun."

"And the sequined boots?" asks Star.

"They belong to my sister," he answers.

Star and Addy exchange glances.

He pauses, then adds, "My sister

is somewhat of a . . . celebrity. Her name is Luna Bright."

"**The Luna Bright?** Who will be performing at the Starlight?" Maya squeals.

Mr. Vertex nods. The students' mouths drop open. They all know about her big hit song, "The Nick of Time."

Mr. Vertex ends by saying, "PS 8 has invited my sister to school the Monday after her concert. That's when Ms. Tempo and I would like you to sing the numbers song. It will be a nice surprise for her, and you can perform the song onstage in the auditorium."

"In front of the whole school?" asks Star.

"Yep," says Mr. Vertex. "I know you can do it, since you've learned the song by heart. My sister will be thrilled. She likes numbers almost as much as I do."

Addy looks around. Everyone seems kind of nervous. Some of the students are probably worried about stage fright. Addy wonders if she'll even have the courage to perform in front of so many people, especially with Luna Bright in the audience.

"Afterward," Mr. Vertex says, looking right at Addy, "Ms. Tempo, my *co-creator*, and I will host a reception. It will be in honor of my sister."

Addy feels as if she might faint. She's so relieved! Everything finally makes sense. She whispers to Star, "I sure learned my lesson."

Star whispers back, "Me too. Better late than never."

8

Time's Up!

When Addy mentions the concert to her mom, her mother immediately orders tickets. Addy asks her dad to come too.

Addy to Dad:

You'll get to see Luna Bright close up!

And our class will perform a special song Mr. Vertex wrote.

Dad to Addy:

I'm taking time off at Christmas for you and me to visit Grand-pop and Grand-mama.

That's all the vacation I can spare right now.

I'm so sorry.

Addy's stomach twists into a pretzel. *Why did he have to move to San Francisco? It's so far away that I hardly ever get to see him.*

On the day of the concert, Addy and her mom sit with Star and Ms. Atlas. Since they get there at

12:45 p.m., forty-five minutes early, Addy counts the number of seats in the ballroom. One thousand! Then she adds and subtracts the rows.

Finally the lights dim. Right on time, at 1:30 p.m., Luna Bright dances onto the stage. Her sequined vest matches her boots. Sparkles rain down from the ceiling. She sings one song after another as her band plays in the background. When she ends the concert with her number one hit, "The Nick of Time," everyone stands up and sings along.

Addy can't wait to meet Luna at the reception the next day. She's so excited, she can't get to sleep, even when she skip counts to one thousand.

< >

On Monday at 1:45 p.m., Mr. Vertex leads his class into the auditorium. A buzz of excitement fills the room. Addy's heart is pounding. *What if I forget the words to the song? What if I trip as I walk onstage?* She glances over at Star, who looks just as worried.

Ten minutes later Mr. Vertex appears with his sister and leads her to a front-row seat.

Then **Ms. Ralston**, the principal, and Mr. Vertex walk to the stage, and everyone quiets down.

"Let's welcome our very special guest, Luna Bright, to PS 8!" Ms. Ralston announces.

The crowd whoops and cheers enthusiastically. And then Mr. Vertex speaks. "I'm so pleased that my sister could join us today."

Things go as smooth as butter,

although Willard sneezes five times on the way up to the stage. But the class remembers every single word to the song, and when they are done performing, Luna gives them a standing **ovation.**

Addy is so thrilled that she blurts out, "Ms. Bright, your brother wrote the words to that song!"

And Star adds, **"And Ms. Tempo wrote the music!"**

Luna's face lights up with a dazzling smile, surprised and proud at this news.

At the reception Addy and Star finally get to meet their favorite singer. When Mr. Vertex introduces them, Addy is tongue-tied at first.

At last, she untwists her tongue enough to ask, "How many years have you been a pop star?"

Luna Bright and Mr. Vertex look at each other, and he gives his sister an encouraging nod.

"Let's see if you can figure it out, Addy. I started performing in 2018. Now it's 2024. So how many years have I been at it?" asks Luna.

Addy quickly subtracts 2018 from 2024. "Six," she utters, then adds, "By the way, I love your boots."

Once again Luna's face lights up with a dazzling smile.

That night Addy lies awake staring at the ceiling. She thinks about all that's happened in the last few weeks.

1. I've learned to tell time and set alarms.

2. I still like to know when things will happen and how long they'll take.

3. Facts matter. Rumors can cause problems.

4. Mr. Vertex isn't getting married.

5. I met Luna Bright in person.

6. I'll get to see Dad at Christmas.

Addy glances at her clock. It's 8:15 p.m. She counts the number of minutes until midnight. She finally falls asleep and dreams about sequined boots.

Word List

analog clock (AN•uh•log KLAWK): A clock that displays time using a short hand to show the hour, a long hand to show minutes, and a skinny hand to show seconds

beckoning (BEH•kuhn•ing): Signaling for someone to come

colon (KOH•luhn): A punctuation mark that looks like one period on top of another

digital clock (DIH•juh•tull KLAWK):

A clock that shows numbers in a row and has a colon between the hour number and the minutes number

lotus (LOH•tuss): A type of flowering plant that lives in the water

lyrics (LIHR•icks): The words to a song

mutters (MUH•turz): Says words or sounds under one's breath

ovation (oh•VAY•shun): Enthusiastic applause for a performance

pawn (PAHN): A piece in the game of chess

precise (prih•SICE): Exact

rectangular (rek•TANG•gyuh•luhr): Shaped like a rectangle

research (REE•surch): Careful and close study

schedule (SKEH•jool): A plan for when actions will take place

sequined (SEE•kwund): Decorated with small shiny discs

startled (STAR•tulled): Suddenly surprised

stumped (STUMPT): Completely puzzled

Questions

1. Do you have more digital clocks or analog clocks at home?
2. Why did Addy think Mr. Vertex was getting married?
3. Did the class sing Mr. Vertex and Ms. Tempo's song in the afternoon?
4. Do you think it was easy for Addy to keep the schedule she created?
5. Do you have a daily schedule?
6. How many seconds are there in a minute and a half?

CHUCKLE YOUR WAY THROUGH THESE EASY-TO-READ ILLUSTRATED CHAPTER BOOKS!

EBOOK EDITIONS ALSO AVAILABLE

FROM ALADDIN
SIMONANDSCHUSTER.COM/KIDS

LOOKING FOR YOUR NEXT FAST, FUN READ? BE SURE TO MAKE IT ALADDIN QUIX!

EBOOK EDITIONS AVAILABLE

ALADDIN • SIMONANDSCHUSTER.COM/KIDS